NOISY BOOKS

READZONE
ReadZone Books Limited

First published in this edition 2015

British Library Cataloguing in Publication Data (CIP) is available for this title.

Printed in Malta by Melita Press.

ISBN 978 1 78322 464 7

Visit our website: www.readzonebooks.com

NOISY BOOKS

Paul Harrison
and Fabiano Fiorin

READZONE

I love the
quiet library.

And all its noisy books.

"ROAR!" goes the dinosaur.

"Shh!" says Mum.

"BOOM!" goes the cannon.

“Shh!” says Mum.

"WHOO!" goes the ghost.

"Shh!" says Mum.

“ZAP!” goes the alien.

"Shh!" says Mum.

Home time.

"WHOOPS!" goes Mum.

"THUD" go the books.

“Shh!” I say.

Did you enjoy this book?

Look out for more *Robins* titles –
first stories in only 50 words

A Head Full of Stories by Su Swallow and Tim Archbold
ISBN 978 1 78322 456 2

Billy on the Ball by Paul Harrison and Silvia Raga
ISBN 978 1 78322 125 7

Countdown! by Kay Woodward and Ofra Amit
ISBN 978 1 78322 462 3

Cave-Baby and the Mammoth by Vivian French and Lisa Williams
ISBN 978 1 78322 126 4

Hattie the Dancing Hippo by Jillian Powell and Emma Dodson
ISBN 978 1 78322 463 0

Molly is New by Nick Turpin and Silvia Raga
ISBN 978 1 78322 455 5

Mr Bickle and the Ghost by Stella Gurney and Silvia Raga
ISBN 978 1 78322 472 2

Noisy Books by Paul Harrison and Fabiano Fiorin
ISBN 978 1 78322 464 7

Not-So-Silly Sausage by Stella Gurney and Liz Million
ISBN 978 1 78322 465 4

The Sand Dragon by Su Swallow and Silvia Raga
ISBN 978 1 78322 127 1

Undersea Adventure by Paul Harrison and Barbara Nascimbeni
ISBN 978 1 78322 466 1

Yummy Scrummy by Paul Harrison and Belinda Worsley
ISBN 978 1 78322 467 8